AMERICAN TOO

Elisa Bartone • Ted Lewin

Lothrop, Lee & Shepard Books   New York

Special thanks to the Lower East Side
Tenement Museum

For J.
E.B.

For all the Italians who have touched my life
T.L.

WHEN ROSINA ARRIVED in New York Harbor, the first thing she saw was the Statue of Liberty. "*Che bella!*" she said—how beautiful! "I want to wear a dress like that, and have a crown, and carry a torch, and have my own book."

"*Tutt' è possibile in America,*" Rosina's mother answered—anything is possible in America.

Rosina grew up believing this with her whole heart—and that anything was possible for her.

Then one day on her way to Aunt Tomasina's chicken market on Broome Street, a group of girls blocked her path. They didn't look friendly.

"What's that you're wearing around your neck?" the tallest one asked.

Rosina fingered the red coral horn she always wore to ward off the evil eye, but she didn't answer.

"She probably doesn't speak English," said a girl with shiny black hair and sky blue eyes.

"She's superstitious," a third girl said, looking straight at Rosina. "It's supposed to do some kind of dumb magic. Don't you know in *America* we don't believe in that?"

Rosina stepped back. She felt her face burn. "I'm American, too!" she said as evenly as she could.

She turned toward home, determined not to run. The girls' laughter echoed in her ears all the way back to Mulberry Street.

Rosina ran into her building and up the steps, two at a time. She raced to her room, tore off the necklace and threw it against the wall. Then she found her red socks and her red ribbon and threw them, too. "Let Mama wear something red for that old evil eye. Not me. I'm going to *laugh* at it, if I ever get to see it!"

Then Rosina picked up her old rag doll from the bed. "Alessandra, this is America. I'm going to have to call you something new. . . . *Meghan O'Hara*," she said finally. "A good American name."

The next morning Rosina and her brother Frankie sat in the kitchen, dipping biscotti into cups of warm milk, coffee, and sugar. Rosina stirred the drink, her head bent, her dark eyes raised to watch Mama making lunch for school.

"It's eggplant," said Rosina. "I hate eggplant."

"You *love* eggplant, Rosina," said Mama.

"That was before," Rosina told her. "American girls don't eat eggplant for lunch. And you must never call me Rosina again. Now I'm Rosie, a modern American girl."

"Sì, ROSIE," said Mama, folding her arms across her chest. "Now take your lunch."

Rosie took the lunch, but she did not intend to eat it.

That afternoon, there was company.

"If you've got to have Jimmy over all the time, make him stop gawking at me, Frankie," Rosie whispered to her brother.

Frankie laughed. "I'm trying to find you a husband," he teased.

"I'm too young for a husband," Rosie told him, "and when I want one, I'll pick him out myself. Someone like Rudolph Valentino. No neighborhood boys for me!"

Frankie rolled his eyes.

Rosie watched her family and Jimmy carefully. Their hands gestured as they spoke—in Italian.

"Why are you sitting on your hands, Rosie?" asked Jimmy, in Italian.

"I don't know," Rosie answered, in English.

"Rosina, wait till you hear," said Papa. "Soon will be the feast of San Gennaro. And this year, you are going to be the queen."

Mama smiled. Frankie and Jimmy whistled and whooped.

Rosie swallowed. "I can't," she said.

"What does that mean, you can't?" Papa asked. "It's an honor to be the queen."

Rosie jumped from her chair. "It's an Italian feast. It's . . . it's not modern. And you're not asking me, you're telling me. In America, the kids are supposed to be free. And why do we always have to do Italian things? This is America, not Italy!" Then she bolted from the room before her father could answer.

Rosie ran down the stairs and out of the building. She ran and ran as far as she could, straight down Broadway toward the water, until she could see the Statue of Liberty in the harbor. All she could think was, "How can I show everyone I'm *really* American?"

She gazed at the lady for a long time. Suddenly a big smile lit Rosie's face. "Thank you!" she shouted. Then she started the long walk back.

When Rosie got home, she was ready for a scolding, but no one said a word. She was so tired, she fell on her bed. "Alessandra . . . I mean Meghan," Rosie whispered, "there's going to be a surprise at the feast this year!"

All week before the feast, Rosie could barely contain her excitement. By Friday, she hardly recognized Mulberry Street. The shopkeepers had decorated their windows, each trying to outdo the other. The Nardi bakery had flowers and bread baked in wonderful shapes—stars, chickens, and crescent moons.

Romeo's pasticcerìa had beautiful displays of pastry—cannoli, babá rum, and cassatine. Brightly colored bunting festooned the windows.

In Donna Concetta's maccheróni store there were pictures of the Saint and votive candles and baskets and jars of pasta in every shape you could imagine. Rosie found the ones she liked best: conchigliette (little shells), cappèlletti (little hats), nocchette (little bows), ruote (wagon wheels), and farfalle (butterflies).

In DePalma's latticini store, there were provolone the size of baseballs, provolone the size of cantaloupes, and long giant ones, hanging from string. Some were shaped like little pigs.

Armando's restaurant had a cannon outside the door.

"You're not going to fire that, are you, Signor Armando?" Rosie called.

"No, Rosie, it's just for show," he answered.

Don Ciccio's restaurant had Italian and American flags, banners, and a figure of San Gennaro.

On the corner, men were building a shrine. Rosie closed her eyes for a second and imagined the beautiful flowers and votive candles that would be there soon.

The band was practicing in Don Ciccio's courtyard. Rosie tapped her feet. She listened for the clarinet, the piccolo, the trombone, and the drums. She wanted to stay, but she had to go home and work on her surprise.

More than once, Rosie heard the door creak.

"Frankie, is that you?" she called. "Go away. This is a secret!"

At last it was Saturday—the day of the feast. All Rosie's neighbors and friends put on their best clothes and walked to the eleven o'clock mass.

"Papa, let's go!" she shouted.

"Now you can't wait," Papa teased her.

After mass, the men, young and old, carried the statue of San Gennaro from the church to the shrine they had built. People lit candles and pinned money onto streamers that hung from the statue and the shrine. They made their wishes.

"I want to be *modern*," Rosie said softly as she pinned a dollar on. "*Really* American."

All day long people strolled along arm in arm, talking and laughing and stopping to eat their favorite foods at the tables the shopkeepers had set up on the sidewalks. Rosie had zeppole, lemon ice, and chocolate gelato.

There were games in the streets. Rosie saw her uncles Giacomo and Giuseppe, Grandpa Grande and Grandpa Franco playing bocce.

And there was Maria, telling fortunes with a deck of cards. "Me next, all right, Maria?" Rosie pleaded.

"In a few years, Rosie. Your father wouldn't like it," Maria told her.

"Please, Maria?" Rosie begged. "Let's do it anyway."

Maria laughed. "You're going to have a wonderful life!" she called as Rosie skipped away.

"I know!" Rosie shouted back.

The shopkeepers exchanged gifts of food. Pasquale Nardi gave Papa a giant sheet cake piled high with whipped cream and decorated with sugar roses and candied fruit. Rosie ate a big piece.

"If I eat one more thing, I'll burst!" she said, and plopped down on a stoop.

Then it was time to get ready.

At five o'clock, the procession formed at the shrine on the corner. The band began to play—time to call for the queen of the feast and her princesses!

The musicians led the way, followed by the statue of San Gennaro, held high on the men's shoulders. It seemed as if everyone in the neighborhood was joining the parade.

First the band stopped in front of each of the princesses' buildings and played until they came out. They called for Nanninella, they called for Graziella, they called for Antonella, they called for Gabriella, Carmela, Amelia, Annunziata, and finally Elisabetta.

The princesses walked two by two, with all the marchers following, to the last building—home of the queen. The band played below Rosie's window and waited for her to come down.

Rosie peeked outside. Mama and Papa and Frankie were waiting for her with the crowd in the street below. She took one last look at herself in the long white taffeta dress Mama had made, and she glanced at the sparkling crown on the dresser. Her stomach flopped and her heart skipped a beat. Then she took a deep breath and reached under the bed for the box that held her surprise.

"Here comes the queen!" someone said, and the children clapped and shouted. Then Rosie stepped outside, dressed as the Statue of Liberty!

The band stopped playing and everyone stared. Rosie thought the silence would last forever. She told Elisabetta, the smallest princess, "I'm *modern*. I'm *really* American now," and touched her crown to make sure it would not fall off. The little girl grinned and said, "I want a book and a torch and a crown, just like Rosie's!" The crowd cheered, and the band started up again.

The procession left Rosie's building—the shopkeepers, the band, the saint, the princesses, and Rosie. Everyone who wanted to march fell in line. "That's my sister," Rosie heard Frankie brag.

They walked to Spring Street, then around to Mott, stopping whenever someone flagged down the statue to pin money on. The more money someone gave, the longer the band stayed and played. People threw confetti and flowers from fire escapes and windows. Some threw dollar bills. Rosie held the torch high through it all.

They marched down Hester Street and arrived back at the shrine. The statue was set in its place. The band moved to the bandstand, where the singers were waiting. People were dancing in the streets. Someone tapped Rosie on the shoulder, and she turned around. It was Uncle Sam! Rosie looked closer.

"Jimmy!" she said. "Why are you dressed like that?"

"I knew Lady Liberty would not refuse to dance with Uncle Sam!" Jimmy answered.

Rosie laughed. "Anything is possible in America," she told him. Rosie took a long look around her. "I'm glad we didn't leave the feast in Italy," she said.

"The good things, we keep," said Jimmy.

"Like presents . . ." Rosie began.

". . . from Italy to America!" Jimmy said happily.

Rosie smiled. Then Jimmy led her to join the dancers, as fireworks lit up the sky.